Tog
the
Dog

Colin and

Jacqui Hawkins

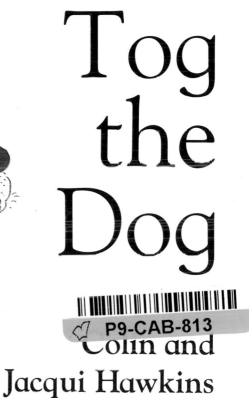

DK

DORLING KINDERSLEY
London • New York • Stuttgart

Have you heard of Tog the dog?

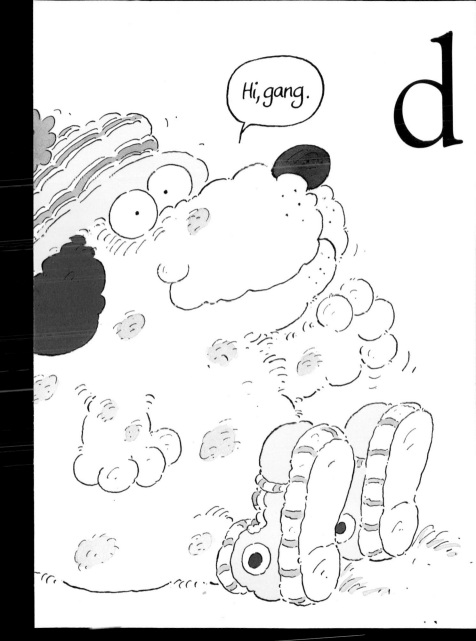

One day Tog went out
for a jog.

He got lost in a fog,

tripped over a cog,

and frightened a frog.

Along came a fat hog,

h

who picked up a log,

1

and pulled out of the bog
the dog called Tog.

A DORLING KINDERSLEY BOOK

Published in the United Kingdom in 1995
by Dorling Kindersley Limited,
9 Henrietta Street, London WC2E 8PS

Published in the United States in 1995
by Dorling Kindersley Publishing, Inc.,
95 Madison Avenue, New York, New York 10016

2 4 6 8 10 9 7 5 3

ISBN 0-7513-5353-1 (UK)
ISBN 0-7894-0176-2 (US)

Reproduction by DOT Gradations
Printed in Italy by L.E.G.O.